TWEEZER
& OTHER STORIES

R. H. DIXON

CORVUS CORONE PRESS

Front cover by Carrion Crow Design.

Corvus Corone Press.

For commuters everywhere.

Other books by R. H. Dixon

Novels:
Emergence
A Storytelling of Ravens
Cribbins
The Shadow of a Shadow

The Sullivan Carter Series:
The Cundy (Book #1)
The Weeper (Book #2)

Novellas:
The Muse

Short Story Collections:
The Unfamiliar & Other Stories

'This ain't no technological breakdown, oh no, this is the road to hell.'
Chris Rea

R. H. DIXON

Contents

R. H. DIXON

Foreword

For most of 2021 and 2022, my morning commute, on a good day, was forty minutes. I listened to the radio, alternating between stations, depending what tunes were playing and what the presenters were talking about, as it gave me a sense of being connected with the world. Anything might have happened overnight while I'd slept, after all.

As I'm at my most creative first thing on a morning, I wanted to make better use of the time spent travelling to work because it felt wasted. So, I came up with a plan to take the first line of the first song I heard on the radio – however good or bad – and think up a loose story idea based on those words.

Straight away, I enjoyed doing this daily mental exercise. Each sentence prompt got me thinking outside the box, encouraging me to consider themes and possibilities I otherwise might not have.

Keen to develop the idea further, I asked my readers on social media if they'd like to get involved by giving me a one-word prompt. I'd then team this word with the first line of the first radio song of the day to give me the starting point for a story – a story I promised my readers I'd make them the star of.

So here we are. This collection is the first instalment of that project. Ten bite-sized stories dreamt up while travelling the ever-busy dual carriageway each day; driving too fast or not moving at all, but always imagining a world far beyond the nine-till-five routine I was headed towards.

Tweezer

It's a warm day. Warm enough for short sleeves and cold lemonade in the garden. Two midges skate on the surface of Heather's fizzy pop. Three others have drowned in it. Birds chatter somewhere not too far away and there's a distant burr of someone's lawnmower. Every now and then, Heather's smartphone pings with some new notification; text message, email, social media post, breaking news, some reminder which she may or may not have set. She ignores the phone's alerts. Is kneeling on the flagstones, smelling of coconut sunscreen and tending to the flowerbed that runs the length of the lawn.

There's a selection of wallflowers, pansies and geraniums; an explosion of colour. Weeds which seem to have grown overnight mar their joyful effect, however. Heather wraps her hand around one of the weeds and pulls. There's some resistance before it uproots and breaks free from the soil. White stuff oozes from its broken stem like craft glue, sticking to her fingers.

Heather frowns. There are countless more to tackle.

She rubs her claggy hands together and thinks about how she hasn't seen weeds like these before. Tall with thorny, blackish stalks and bulbous, spiky heads, she's not even sure they are weeds. But she didn't plant them and thinks they're ugly, so presumes that's what they must be.

It takes Heather almost two hours to remove, bag and bin them all. After which, her hands are beyond sticky with their residue. Back hurting and knees aching, she stands in the middle of the lawn to admire the now unobstructed view of flowers. But instead of feeling satisfied, Heather's strangely troubled. Has an urgency to go inside and wash her hands. To scrub them with a scouring pad and strong detergent till they're pink and raw. Because if she doesn't…

She doesn't know.

There's an uncomfortable, irrational idea scratching around in her mind. It's not fully formed but has barbed hooks and sharp baby teeth filled with milky poison, scraping at her sensibilities. Reminding her she's…

She's…

She's…

She can't think straight.

That the weeds' essence is seeping into her pores creates a building sense of panic. Because if she doesn't get it off her skin, she'll be… what?

Tainted?

Heather runs into the house and washes her hands till they sting. Watery blood sits in the creases of her fingers. She eyes the garden from the kitchen window as though it's a familiar but unwanted visitor. It's weed-free now, but she doesn't like the memory of how it had looked earlier in the day. All that black twine. She pulls the roller blind down, so she doesn't have to see where it was. Her hands are clean, but she feels unclean on some deeper level she can't pinpoint. The inkling is altogether too dangerous. Her hands don't look like her own, and she considers maybe they aren't.

Too much sun and no hat and not enough water, she thinks.

Her smartphone jingles with a new alert. Annoyed by its intrusion, Heather activates the smartphone's silent mode.

Later that day, Heather's at work. A new customer

needs registering in the system.

'Waste of my bloody time, this is,' he says. 'Let me just pay my money and go in. I know what I'm doing. Read up about all the equipment online already.' He waves his smartphone in the air, as if this is proof enough that he's an expert.

'Sorry, sir, but I must register you before you can use the facilities.'

'But why? It's absurd.'

'It's the rules. It'll only take a few minutes. Then I'll need to sort out an induction for you.'

The man rolls his eyes and huffs like a petulant child.

As Heather passes a registration form over the counter for him to jot down his personal details and fitness goals, a stabbing pain in the meaty flesh of her left palm causes her to suck air in through her teeth.

'Did you just hiss at me?' the man asks. His expression suggests he's already decided to make a formal complaint against her. She knows his type well. One of life's constant complainers. Nothing's ever good enough. Everything's an inconvenience. He thinks the world revolves around him.

'No. Sorry. I didn't.' Heather looks at her hand and sees there's a black speck trapped beneath the skin. She scratches the area with her nail, but it doesn't look like it'll come out easily.

'It's just a spelk I got while gardening,' she explains, showing him. As if he'd care. 'I'll get it out later.'

But by the time Heather gets home, after an influx of other unsatisfied, self-absorbed customers, she's forgotten about the spelk. She makes dinner for her family, then washes up. Everyone spends the evening scrolling through newsfeeds and watching videos on their smartphones, their faces lit up. No one asks how her day was. No one mentions the garden, to say it looks better or to thank her for spending so much of her time out there.

'Look at this,' her son says, angling his smartphone so Heather can see its screen. 'You'll love it, it's hilarious.'

Heather watches a video that's playing on some social media platform. Someone has dressed their dog in a tutu and buckled it, like a child, into a pushchair, which is being wheeled around the garden by their toddler who's wearing a nappy. Heather neither loves it nor thinks it's funny. In fact, she wishes she hadn't seen it at all. Poor dog looks as miserable as she feels.

Her son can't understand why she doesn't find it funny.

She can't understand why he does.

That night Heather has restless dreams about a blackness that covers the house like thick, dripping tar. She's trapped inside and can't get out and watches as the mysterious substance seeps through the gaps around the front and back door, crawling along the carpet, filling corners and oozing along skirting boards. Soon, the inky black climbs the interior walls, seeking to take over. Whatever it is, she feels it's not only organic but sentient, too. Filled with such negativity, it'll consume and destroy everything in its path.

The next day Heather's at the supermarket, waiting to checkout. A woman jumps into the queue ahead, as though her time is more important than everyone else's and no one will notice or challenge her, and the man behind nudges Heather's backside with his trolley. Heather turns her head to see if it was an accident. Maybe the man will offer an apology.

He doesn't.

The man seems completely oblivious, too busy tapping away on the screen of his smartphone.

Heather grips the handle of her heavy shopping basket tighter and is aware that her palm is throbbing. Switching the basket to her other hand, she looks and sees the flesh is reddened and tender around the spelk. Infected, perhaps.

As soon as she gets home, Heather dumps her shopping bags on the kitchen floor and inspects her hand. The spelk is very much embedded, the surrounding flesh inflamed. She searches for a needle, then scrapes at the top layer of skin, poking deeper, trying to bring the spelk to the surface. But it's not coming. From inside her handbag on the counter, her phone starts ringing. And she hears the dog coughing and hacking in the lounge as though he's being sick.

'Not on the carpet,' she cries, rushing through, ignoring the phone.

Too late.

She finds a pile of black, slimy sludge waiting on the cream carpet. The dog's lying next to it; ears flat to his head, eyes glassy.

'It's okay,' she tells him calmly, despite her utter dismay that the carpet might be stained. 'I'll clean it up. It's okay.'

Heather realises as she scoops the vomit into a poly bag that it contains long strands of black weed, the type she'd pulled from the garden the day before. She can't understand how it came to be that the dog had eaten some. He's not prone to eating stuff he shouldn't and, besides, she'd put all the weeds in the garden waste bin.

She sprays carpet cleaner on the dark patch. Then, hoping it'll work magic, goes back to the kitchen where she picks up the needle again. Gouging at the flesh of her palm, she tries with renewed vigour to fish out the spelk. The wound is raw and oozes clear liquid. But she's too anxious to care. Needs this foreign object out of her.

The spelk is blacker and more accessible now she's worked the overlaying skin, but it's still too awkward to tease out with the needle. Heather fetches her cosmetic bag from the bathroom and rummages inside to find her tweezers. Confident these will do the trick, she grips the tip of the spelk and feels a swell of satisfaction when she pulls and feels it dislodge and break free.

But then…

No. It's longer than she'd thought and very much still burrowed in her hand. When she tugs again, a strange sensation runs down her entire arm. A lightning zap of nerve pain.

The underside of her face flashes cold.

Her smartphone starts ringing again.

shutupshutupshutupshutup

She pulls at the spelk with the tweezers while thinking: get out, get out, get out, get out. And her phone beeps to notify she has a new voicemail. And she can hear the dog being sick again. But she can't go to him because she has her own crisis to deal with. She yanks and watches more black twine unravel from her hand like a loose thread.

Still, it doesn't break free.

Her smartphone hums with a new alert. There's always someone hounding her; seeking her attention, trying to sell her stuff she doesn't need, wanting something from her, even just time.

Just time. Ha!

She takes a deep breath and pulls with the tweezers. More twine feeds out of her hand, and this time she feels an uncomfortable pulling sensation course down her leg. She imagines the twine has spread throughout her body, growing and wrapping around her bones.

Again, she pulls with the tweezers.

GET OUT.

Her fingers jolt involuntarily, as though the tendons in her arm have been squeezed by an unseen hand. The dog comes into the kitchen, cowering. He vomits more black sludge onto the lino. Heather turns and opens the back door to let him into the garden. Needs some fresh air. Feels lightheaded. But when she glimpses the garden, she feels even fainter.

The weeds are back.

They've taken over the flowerbed again and are sprouting from the cracks in the pavement and climbing the walls of the house. An intricate network of black twine seeking to take over. The same hateful black twine that's unravelling from her hand.

Growing and growing and growing.

Beep.

Wine

The lift slides up its shaft smoothly, the way it ought to. Yet, for Mark, it tilts from side to side in the way all rooms do when you've had too much to drink. Music plays from unseen speakers; a piano rendition of some famous song Mark can't quite place. Something about an umbrella, perhaps, that pokes at his brain. He tries not to look at any of the mirrored walls that surround him, because they're creating the illusion that he's in a box within a box within a box, ad infinitum. Not only might the visual trickery make him vomit, but his face is dripping with blood and he doesn't want to see. It's on his hands and shirt, too.

What the hell happened?

He's hyperventilating.

Thank goodness no one is in the lift with him.

Mark had a couple of glasses of Malbec with his steak, that's it. It's a work's event, after all, and it's a steadfast rule of his not to overdo the booze when socialising with colleagues. Nothing good can ever come of it.

So how did he end up this drunk and out of control?

Was his wine spiked?

He doesn't even want to consider whose blood he's wearing.

The company he works for roped fifty members of staff into a 'team-building' and 'morale-boosting' exercise; archery and axe-throwing within a fancy hotel's extensive grounds during the day, followed by a slap-up meal in its five-star restaurant in the evening and an overnight stay.

Funnily enough, Mark can't recall much of the daytime activities. Disturbing snippets arise now and then, confusing him with a realness that's brutal and graphic, yet impossible. Leoni, the apprentice, is looking at Mark and screaming, her face stippled red, one of her hands missing; Wendy, one of the four office cleaners, is holding one of her shiny leather loafers aloft, which still contains her foot that's been severed at the ankle; and Greg, Mark's team leader, has an axe wedged in his skull. When Mark tries to force the disgusting, false memories further to the surface, they retreat deeper into his subconscious where they can't be reached. Only when he doesn't try to gain access to them do they tease him with bold familiarity.

Nothing so terrible could have happened to Leoni, Wendy and Greg, though, Mark reasons. There'd be way too much disruption and hysteria for Mark to have gone on to spend a mundane evening dining with Dee from HR, Nick from Procurement and Jeff from Finance. Surely, he'd have given a statement to the police earlier in the day, then gone home, the 'morale-boosting' awayday completely ruined and unsalvageable, and tuned into Look North to see if the bloodbath got a teatime mention. Instead, he'd suffered Dee with her many rambling anecdotes, Nick with his cough, a controlled *aghm-aghm* into his rolled hand, a pre-warner for whenever he was about to speak, mostly about his self-important achievements, but sometimes about his kids who sounded every bit as insufferable as he was, and Jeff's unnerving zombie-stare. Mark hadn't been able to decide if Jeff was stoned or simply bored.

When the elevator pings to announce its arrival on the twentieth floor, Mark stumbles into the corridor. The walls are a tube of pulsing, pink muscle that an axe blade or arrowhead could easily perforate, and the floor is a channel of freshly spilt blood…

Mark groans.

Pink wallpaper. Red carpet. That's all.

Why is there so much carnage in his head?

He pats at his pockets to find his room card. There are no numbers on it, but he remembers he's staying in 2020; second room from the end on the right. It's the name of the fortified wine he and his mates used to buy from the off-licence when he was a teenager. Mad Dog 2020, they'd called it. He associates it with drunkenness, which seems quite apt. It's also the cursed year of Covid, of course. No matter how drunk, no one's going to forget that in a hurry.

Mark finds room 2020 and fiddles with his key card, sliding it into the slot on the door handle's lock mechanism. A green light flashes and he hears a click. He opens the door and falls into the room.

'Hello, Mark.' A man in a black suit is standing by the bed. He looks familiar, but not. 'Did you enjoy that little illusion I created for you?'

'Er…?' Mark staggers towards the bed. Needs to sit. Fights the urge to vomit. He sees the man's wearing a badge on his jacket, engraved with the hotel's logo. 'Who are you? And why are you in my room?'

The man places a hand on Mark's shoulder. 'I'm an illusionist.' Then he snaps his fingers.

°○°° .*. °○○°

Mark opens his eyes. He's lying in a cold, dark space that's much smaller than he thinks it should be. It's certainly not his hotel room.

The back of a van, perhaps?

Everything's still spinning. He tries to move but can't. Then realises his arms and legs are bound.

'Hello again, Mark.' It's the illusionist. He's hunkered in the space next to Mark's head. 'You'll be pleased to know your practice runs are over. I especially enjoyed this time around. You're getting very good at it. Quite the creative one.'

The man's face, perhaps even his identity, is buried somewhere in Mark's thoughts, mingling amongst the unreachable spatter-gore memories of Leoni and Wendy's severed appendages and Greg's smashed skull. An idea of who the man is tries to surface, but its vagueness affords Mark only a fleeting mental image of the man handing an axe to him. Then the memory, or whatever it is, dissolves.

'The way you stabbed Dee from HR in the eye with your fork, then slit Nick from Procurement's throat with his own wine glass, before shoving Jeff from Finance's steak knife through his temple, all in a matter of seconds, was way more original than our axe training earlier,' the illusionist says. 'It was such a rush. I bet the adrenaline was good for you, too, huh? Better than an orgasm. You have a flair for violence. A certain… je ne sais quoi. Now let's have some real fun and make things even more dramatic. More grotesque. Because I like dramatic-grotesque. It turns me on.'

What the hell are you talking about? Mark wants to ask. But the words won't form. He's unable to speak. Unable to move. Only his mind runs freely.

Or does it?

What earlier axe training?

He thinks of Leoni, Wendy and Greg. Fights his gag reflex, because what if…

'I've left a petrol chainsaw behind the potted tree in the hotel foyer.' The illusionist winks. 'You'll know what to do.'

Mark's eyes widen. 'Wha…?'

'When I say sleep,' the illusionist says, 'you'll go to sleep. Then when I click my fingers, you'll become the brazen killer again, but for real this time. At the mention of wine, you'll want to mess up Dee from HR, Nick from Procurement and Jeff from Finance good and proper. Then you'll wipe out the entire call centre crew, bunch of fuckers that they are.'

'Why are you doing this to me?' Mark's heart is thumping.

The illusionist smiles. 'Sleep.'

Snap.

°○°.*.°○°

Mark jolts from a daze. He's standing outside the fancy hotel. There's a mild breeze, and it's starting to drizzle. He feels dizzy. Nauseous, even. Must be the wine, he thinks. He can't remember coming outside. But figures he must have popped out for some fresh air. Maybe to escape his colleagues' patter, which, if Mark's being honest, is utterly tedious.

'Alright, sir?'

Mark turns and sees a man in a black suit. Must be a hotel worker. There's a badge with its logo affixed to his lapel. 'Er, yeah, thanks.' Something about the man gnaws at Mark's intuition like a subliminal message. Something that…

Nope, it's gone.

Perhaps he looks like someone famous.

'Are you enjoying yourself?'

'Hmn. Suppose so.' Mark sighs. Then he laughs. What's the point in lying? 'Nah, not really.' It's been a lousy evening. Hell, the entire day has been a write off. He can barely remember a thing since getting off the coach that morning and being greeted by…

'Can I get you some more wine?' the man in the black suit asks. 'Would that help?'

Mads Mickelson, Mark thinks. That's who he looks like, if I squint. 'Hmmm, wine. Argentinian Malbec?'

The man opens the door, his dark eyes sparking, and gestures for Mark to go inside. 'Certainly, sir.'

Mark smiles appreciatively. It's about time he rejoins his dinner companions, because he doesn't know how long he's been gone and they're probably wondering where he is.

First though, he thinks, as he steps into the bright foyer, there's something I need to pick up. Something behind that potted tree over there.

Ritual

'Today let's talk frothy coffee,' Jolie Fille Folle says, grinning as though the entire world is her willing audience and enthralled by everything she has to say.

Dave's not sure he needs to hear about frothy coffee, but he continues to watch and listen. Can't not. He considers he might be addicted to this girl who's not even French.

Jolie Fille Folle has a voluminous mane of blonde hair that hangs to her tiny, tidy waist. Probably not all of the hair's her own; nylon doll's hair or someone else's hair infused with her own darker roots. She touches and swishes it too much as though she's not used to it being there, tickling her bare arms and back. Perhaps if it belonged to someone else, Dave thinks, they might feel the ghost of it on their skin.

The sky's still pink, not that Jolie Fille Folle would know. She's too wrapped up in herself, slinking about in the familiar chrome kitchen, while angling a smartphone at her face as she goes about making frothy coffee in a pan on the hob. Her voice has a thick-as-treacle huskiness as she speaks to her captive audience, and it's this quality that makes her stand out from the rest. She's a modern-day kind of perfect with her golden-enhanced skin, bleached teeth, synthetic eyelashes, tattooed eyebrows and plump, chemical lips. But her husky voice is natural, and it's *this* that gives her a quirky edge, attracting thousands and thousands more followers than others just like her who try their hand at this same endeavour. Her voice that captures people with the catchphrase: Today let's talk…

'The health benefits of garlic and blood orange infused tea.'

'The implications of negative behaviour AI might have on our dogs when it starts telling them what to do.'

'The beauty secrets found within the soil from your grandmother's flowerbed, especially if it's rich in manure.'

Dave's heard it all.

And he hates himself for finding Jolie Fille Folle so enthralling. Her daily routine is banal, yet strangely mesmeric.

Jolie Fille Folle, she gets in your head.

'Today let's talk blah, blah, blah.'

Ah, who cares? But please, do go on.

It's the same thing day in, day out: Jolie Fille Folle wakes and primps, then does some live social media recordings while making breakfast, which is always a chirpy, conversational piece that makes Dave feel nauseous. But he can't not watch. She primps some more after breakfast, then snaps some selfies and uploads them to her social media outlets. Meanwhile, the data server that stores all her selfies warms the ocean it sits in. She takes a few naps, does some more live social media recordings. Has online chats with friends. Takes more selfies. Sings. Makes something for dinner that, whether cheap or lavish, must make a bold statement that shocks or disgusts. Beauty regimes are saved for evenings and are interspersed with online dares from viewers.

This happens day in, day out.

Day in, day out.

Dave's tired and hungry and doesn't know how long he's been here, watching. Can't remember how he came to be here either. His wrists hurt and he can barely move his body. If he turns his head to the side, he can see there are others there, too. Others just like him. Each of them bound to the massive skylight above the familiar chrome kitchen, anchored to this live stage. Pained captives. And all they can do is watch.

Watch the ritual of this pretty, crazy girl below.

Jolie Fille Folle.

R. H. DIXON

Sea Swimming

The single lane winds its way to a small, secluded beach Kirsty saw yesterday when she and her family had driven past. Its wild beauty had drawn her attention like a magnet, promising exclusivity; a place conducive to adventure and daydreams. She'd known as soon as she'd set eyes on it that she had to visit. Preferably alone.

So that's exactly what she's doing now.

The rest of her family are spending the day at the holiday cottage, preparing for the barbecue they'll have later in its ample garden. Kirsty thinks she probably should have stayed to lend a hand – skewer vegetables, marinate chicken thighs, concoct a large bowl of punch that'll make whoever drinks it merry after just one glass – but since arriving the day before, she's felt a powerful urge to explore the beach. It pulls on her senses with such intensity, she can't ignore it. Like an obsession, enticing and hypnotic, she can't shake off. Even when she'd lain in bed last night, she could hear the waves, imagined or not, a constant lure that had shushed her thoughts; quietening the chaotic jumble of stresses and demands, however trivial, that drain her most days.

A couple of hours of indulgent self-love is all she's asking for.

And her family hadn't objected when she'd voiced her plan.

It's taken ten minutes for Kirsty to walk to the beach, along the single lane. There's a spring in her step and a smile on her face. No cars have passed by, and there are no other signs of people.

Pure bliss.

The strengthening tang of salty sea air is all-enticing, and the sun is warm on her face. Gulls flicker above the sea like white sparks in the distance. The sand looks yellower and the sky bluer than they really are behind the lenses of Kirsty's sunglasses. Everything about the day feels idyllic.

There's a beach towel, a paperback and a flask of hot tea in her backpack. All favourable items for creating a perfect morning, she thinks. And beneath her clothes, she's wearing a swimming costume. Already she's decided, if the sea's not too choppy, she'll take a dip. Can't wait to feel the fresh saltwater against her skin and, subsequently, anticipates being able to taste the delicious salt on her lips during the walk back to the holiday cottage, her face tightened by it.

Her mother said the family had visited this place many years ago, but Kirsty doesn't remember. She wonders if she was as drawn to the beach then as she is now. Can't see how she wouldn't have been. Kicking her shoes off to enjoy the sand between her toes, there's something about the landscape, the way it looks, the way it smells, the way it feels, that pulls at some distant memory. She can't argue she's been here before. Can feel it deep within. But no flashbacks from that time are forthcoming.

Around fifty metres from the shore, a rock juts out of the sea. It looks large and flat enough to stretch out on. The sea is calm, its gentle waves licking at the shoreline.

Easy peasy, Kirsty thinks, weighing up the distance.

She leaves her backpack and folded clothes on the dry sand, then wades into the water. It's fresh enough to catch her breath, but once her body's submerged, she acclimatises quickly and it's not too bad after all. She lies on her back, star-fished, and trusts the water to keep her afloat.

This is my time, she thinks. Time to connect with me.

For the past six weeks Kirsty's been going to weekly guided meditation sessions at her local community centre. The guide, Audrey, is a lady in her sixties who's most likely tried more than one type of recreational drug in her time, Kirsty thinks, and whose tanned, leathery forearms jangle with colourful bangles and beads whenever she moves. She owns a collection of chiffon scarves which she wears around her neck. Each is boldly printed with what Kirsty imagines is Audrey's chosen spirit animal on any given day, depending what mood she's in. Last week she was evidently feeling the power of the elephant. Sturdy feet grounded. Trunk relaxed.

We're all relaxed.

Kirsty enjoys the sessions well enough. She can imagine Audrey's low voice now, the gentle instructions she'd give if she was here: Imagine every hair follicle on your body. They're yours. They're part of your skin, and you can feel your skin, can't you? They're part of *you*. Now focus on your breathing. Really focus. Because that's you, too. And once you tap into you, you can shut everything else out. All those pesky thoughts that invade your headspace when you don't want them to.

Kirsty closes her eyes.

Focus. This is me. My skin. My organs. My hair. My nails. I'm connecting with me.

But as Kirsty concentrates, she's more aware of the sea than she is of herself. Her submerged ears are deafened by its muffled murk, and its waves that lap over her body, albeit gently, are colder than she'd initially thought. The more she tries to appeal to her own consciousness, goosebumps stir on her arms and legs making her shiver.

Focus, she tells herself sternly. This is me. I'm lying in the sun's rays and it's perfectly warm. I'm connecting with *me*.

And yet, she's still more in tune with the sea than herself. In fact, all she can think about is its vastness. Stretching far and deep, parts of it as unknowable and black as space. And all the stuff within it and beneath her which she can't see that might swallow her whole or chew her up with any amount of sharp teeth.

Kirsty opens her eyes, panicked by how much this little exercise has unnerved her. It's never happened before. And she doesn't want this fleeting, irrational fear of the sea to taint her morning with negative vibes, so she flips over and starts swimming towards the rock. Maybe she can connect with herself on the flat, warm, solid surface.

Audrey's voice again: Imagine there's a door. You grip the handle and push it open. Light instantly spills onto you.

Kirsty angles her face to the sun, feeling its warmth. The sea buffets her playfully. She feels safe again.

This light is yours, Audrey says. It's you. And as you step over the threshold into this brilliant light, into *your* light...

Kirsty has a sudden memory of being here with someone else. Swimming alongside a dark-haired girl. The sun is shining, just as it is now, and they're both laughing.

I did it, she thinks excitedly. I've connected with me.

She's remembered something that was buried deep, deep within, no doubt drowned out by a backlog of too many recent thoughts.

You continue walking through the door and discover that you're on a narrow boardwalk, Audrey says. The wooden panels are warm beneath your bare feet. To each side of the boardwalk is clear, turquoise sea, and in the water you can see...

Me and the dark-haired girl swimming to the rock. It was a race. A game!

Last one there's a dirty rascal, Kirsty remembers shouting.

Kirsty grins, basking in the nostalgia of summers long gone and the freedom of childhood. Long, endless days and quick friendships formed on nothing more than the desire to have fun together. No agendas. No ulterior motives. She's filled with a simple joy she's not felt in a long while. A satisfying inner warmth.

I connected with me again, she thinks, triumphantly. I did it.

When Kirsty arrives at the rock, she heaves herself out of the water and stands tall, arms outstretched. Facing the beach, she shouts, 'I'm the king of the castle.' Because there's no one around to hear and she can be as silly as she likes.

The rock's surface is warm, just as she'd thought. The sea slaps against its sides; a surprisingly hollow sound. Kirsty lies on her back, relishing the sun's heat, and closes her eyes.

At the end of the narrow boardwalk, Audrey says, you see a boat. *This* is your anchor. This is where you will anchor yourself to *you*. Whenever you feel anxious and stressed, this is where you must come. Your own little boat that rocks gently in the sea and...

And...

Kirsty remembers there was a boat here that day when she'd swam with the dark-haired girl, and its memory isn't in any way spiritual or serene. There was a man in the boat; ruddy-cheeked, middle-aged and overweight. His large, rough hands reaching down and grabbing her. Kirsty remembers saltwater stinging her eyes and filling her lungs. A vortex of darkness and panic and splashing; the man's hands gripping her, but something tugging on her legs. A battle of strength. The man had hauled her onto his boat so fiercely, purple bruises had blossomed on her arms straight away.

Kirsty sits upright on the rock, her heart thundering.

What the hell happened that day?

Who was the man in the boat? And what happened to the dark-haired girl?

Remember to anchor, Audrey says. Get into your boat and escape the bombardment of other thoughts competing for attention. Switch them all off. Anchor yourself.

You can do it.

Get in the boat.

Ease down gently.

Sit.

Okay, I'm in the boat.

But it rocks violently to and fro, and my arms and chest hurt and I'm scared and the man's face is so close I can see the spittle on his dark whiskers from when he'd shouted at me and his eyes are intense, scaring me even more and…

And…

Kirsty remembers.

The shock of the memory-blow jolts her; a physical reaction that fills her with a dread so profound her skin prickles in a rash of painful goosebumps. Away from the safety of the shallows, the dark-haired girl's demeanour had changed, Kirsty recalls. They were no longer playing a fun game to see who could reach the rock first. The dark-haired girl had grabbed Kirsty's arms, raking her flesh with sharp-clawed fingers. Then she'd pushed Kirsty's head underwater, holding her down with frightening, abnormal strength. The rest is a blur of blind panic. Someone – the man in the boat – hauling Kirsty upwards, and the dark-haired girl trying to keep her in the water. But the man was stronger. Kirsty remembers spluttering and coughing on the bevelled floor of the boat, gritty water sloshing all about her, while the man, red-faced and exerted, had spoken angry words that she can't recall. She'd lurched upright, gripping the side of the boat, and peered into the water. It feels like a false memory, because surely it's impossible, but Kirsty is rewarded a mental image of the dark-haired girl twisting to dive into the depths of the sea and, as she does, her lower body breaks the surface of the water, and for all the world Kirsty can see that her bottom half is like that of a fish. Not the shimmering turquoise and pink scales of the mermaid tails that are depicted in fairy tales and cartoons, this one was as grey as a cold January morning, glistening like a knife's edge. The man who'd saved Kirsty's life had pulled her away from the side of the boat, taken her back to dry land, and warned her never to swim in these waters again.

Yet here she is now.

Was she lured by the siren's call all those years ago, and has she fallen for its call again?

Kirsty jumps to her feet, consumed by terror. She looks to the shore, wants nothing more than to be back on the beach, the safety of dry land. It's tantalisingly close, yet still so far.

False memories, she tells herself. That's all. None of it happened. It can't have. I'd never have forgotten something like that.

And yet, trauma has a way of burying itself deep, a self-preservation tactic.

She hears a gargling, throaty sound that's oddly familiar. Then two hands appear on the rock's ledge with long, needly fingers. A dark-haired woman with pale, almost translucent skin draws herself upwards.

Kirsty feels lightheaded. 'You are real.'

The dark-haired girl grown – an actual mermaid? – has cruel eyes that glint gunmetal in the sun, and when she grins at Kirsty's acknowledgement, her teeth are barbed needles. Funnily enough, these carnivorous teeth hadn't bothered Kirsty when she was a kid. Yet now, they absolutely terrify her.

Anchor yourself, Kirsty hears Audrey say.

'But there's no boat,' Kirsty whines.

The nightmarish creature from her childhood makes a clacking noise in its throat, and its soulless fish's eyes glint hungrily.

Forget the boat, Audrey says. Let the rock be your anchor. The boat's just a symbol. A mental prompt. That's all it ever was. It can be anything you want. Anchor yourself now. Quick!

Kirsty grits her teeth. She's stronger now she's fully grown, and this time she has the advantage of not being in the water. She'll be able to put up a better fight. Sooner or later, her family will come looking for her. All she must do is defend the rock till then.

'Because I'm the king of the castle,' Kirsty says. She stamps down on those needly fingers that are too close to her feet, grinding them into the hard surface of the rock with her heel. The creature shrieks, a banshee wail, and lurches backwards. Kirsty feels grounded and strong. She swings her leg round, drawing power from the rock and using her core strength to smash the creature in the face with her foot. 'And you're the dirty rascal.'

The rock is my anchor.

It's part of me.

The rock *is* me.

Pease Pudding

Paul's late for work. He got stuck in traffic on the A19; multiple pile-ups caused by surface water from the freak storm that hit just before eight and general bad driving. Commuters going too slow or too fast and making hasty, reckless decisions with not enough braking distance between themselves and the vehicle in front. Way too much rubbernecking around the sites of the collisions too. Sheer carnage.

The rain's coming down heavier than Paul thinks he's ever seen it. The sky's end-of-the-world-black. He finds a parking bay at the far side of the office car park, then gets soaked as he dashes to the office's main entrance which feels at least a mile away.

A flash of lightning lights the sky spectral-white as he pushes the door to the foyer open and tumbles inside. A subsequent roll of thunder makes the windows and glass doors vibrate. His shirt sticks to him like a second layer of skin and his socks squelch inside his shoes.

Well, shit, he thinks. Today's gonna be fun.

Usually, Paul uses the stairs to get to his office on the second floor, but this morning he goes straight to the lift. The meeting he's supposed to attend and participate in, something to do with KPIs and organisational restructuring and departmental streamlining, is due to start in less than ten minutes. He's not at all prepared. With his wet forefinger, he jabs at the lift's button multiple times, aware that it won't make the lift arrive any sooner, but needing to express his urgency, nonetheless. He's relieved when the lift pings and its doors open. Once inside the small, mirrored compartment, he presses the button marked '2'. The button lights up green, so he doesn't press it again. Is content that he'll soon be on his way. As the doors slide closed, however, the lift pings and the doors swoosh open again.

A woman with greying dark hair and a bristly upper lip peers inside, says, 'Wait up,' then negotiates a trolley that's piled high with sandwiches into the small space, hemming Paul into the back corner. The woman stocky and must be over six foot tall, he suddenly feels very confined. And remembers, he's left his lunch in the car.

'You're a bit wet,' the woman says, eyeing Paul as if he might not have noticed this detail.

Paul resists rolling his eyes. 'Put my clothes on before taking a shower this morning to change things up a bit, you know?'

The woman snorts. 'Oh, got a funny one, have we?'

Paul inhales deeply, a disguised (or not) impatient sigh. 'Would you mind pressing 'two' for me, please?' The button for the second floor is no longer illuminated green.

'Sure, darl. I'm Barbara, by the way. The sandwich lady.' She makes no attempt to press any of the lift's buttons, and Paul's too far away to be able to reach them himself.

'I didn't realise we have a sandwich lady,' he says. 'But I'm kinda late for a meeting, so if you wouldn't mind.' He tips his head, gesturing the lift's control panel.

'Oh, of course.' Barbara presses '2' then '9', her eyes not leaving Paul. 'Fancy a ham and pease pudding sandwich?'

'Nah thanks. What else do you have?'

'That's the only option, darl.'

'Why?' Paul looks at the mountain of cellophane

wrapped sandwiches. 'That's an awful lot of ham and pease pudding. What if people don't like ham and pease pudding sandwiches?'

Barbara shrugs. 'Tough luck, I'd say. Did you know you can't get pease pudding down south?'

Who gives a fuck? We don't live down south, Paul wants to say, but instead tells her, 'I'm sure you can if you look in the right places.'

'No, I'm telling you, it's as elusive as Bigfoot poo.'

'I'm pretty sure Bigfoot poo is elusive up north too.'

Barbara glares at him.

The lift's not moving and Paul's increasingly aware of his cold, wet clothing, and the smell of pease pudding and the sandwich woman's unwanted attention. 'Could you knock that button again, please? We don't seem to be moving.'

Barbara touches the '2' and '9' buttons again. They're already green, so nothing changes. She picks up a sandwich from her trolley, unwraps it, then pulls the two slices of white bread apart. 'Do you know how pease pudding is made?'

'With peas?'

'Yellow split peas, to be more precise. They're cooked with ham hock and vegetables, then mashed together to form this gorgeous consistency.'

'Fascinating,' Paul says, dryly. He's about to ask if he can get out of the lift to take the stairs when the lift shudders and moves upwards.

Thank Christ.

'It's been around in the Northeast of England since the 14th century, you know.' Barbara scrapes her finger through the pease pudding that's spread thickly on the sandwich she's holding. She puts her finger to her mouth to lick it off. All the while her attention doesn't leave Paul.

Paul shifts uncomfortably. Looks at the ceiling.

Is she trying to be seductive?

Please God, no.

'You know those hospital programmes when someone's having liposuction and you get to see all the fat draining out of 'em?' Barbara says. 'That's what pease pudding reminds me of. All that good yellow, gloopy stuff.'

Paul's mouth downturns. 'And you still want to eat it?'

'Can't get enough of the stuff. Did you know that it used to be known as pease porridge?'

It's suddenly too warm in the lift and all Paul can smell is the damn pease pudding. He pulls at the collar of his shirt, feeling nauseous.

'You alright, darl?' Barbara asks. 'You're looking a little peaky. Why don't you take a bite? It'll make you feel better. Besides, you look like you could do with having more meat on your bones. I like a big man, me.'

'I'm sure you do.' Paul doesn't offer a smile. Feels trapped. 'Look, can you move the trolley to the left a little so I can squeeze past? I need to get out in a second.'

Barbara makes no attempt to move the trolley. 'Go on, treat yourself,' she says, winking. 'Take one from the top. Those have got loads of filling in them.'

Paul shakes his head. 'Nah, I'm good. You didn't exactly sell them to me if I'm being honest.' All he can think of is fat sluicing through tubes on medical documentaries. The ham looks like raw skin.

'Do you know how many people in those crashed cars you passed this morning had pease pudding in their sandwiches for lunch?' Barbara says, shifting her bulky weight from one leg to the other.

'Excuse me?'

'None. Not one single person, that's how many. How tragic is that?'

'How did you know I passed any crashed cars on my

way to work?'

'Popular route.' Barbara shrugs. 'Lucky guess?'

'Whatever.' Paul's had enough of her craziness. Just wants out.

'There were a few fatalities. Not everyone made it out.'

'You definitely couldn't know that. I doubt any of it would have been mentioned on the news yet. Too early.'

Barbara grins. Paul notices she has peculiarly small, sharp teeth. 'I know lots of things, Paul.'

Paul's stance stiffens. How does she know his name?

Maybe he misheard.

Paul, darl – yeah, sounds similar.

'Do you know for certain you made it out alive?' Barbara raises an eyebrow, her eyes glinting with mischief.

Paul snorts forced laughter. 'Are you suggesting I might be dead?'

'Don't be so dramatic. This is just the beginning.'

'Beginning of what? Purgatory?'

Barbara grins, showing him those barbed little teeth.

'I could well believe it,' he mutters.

The '1' button lights up red and the lift judders to a stop.

Paul braces himself. Swallows hard. Something's not right.

There's a deafening clang and the light snaps off, pitching them in total darkness.

'Shit,' Paul says, icy dread filling his veins.

'What's up, darl?' Barbara asks. 'Are you claustrophobic?'

When Paul doesn't answer, he feels the trolley pushing against his legs. Bitch is forcing him farther into the corner.

'There's a very old nursery rhyme about pease pudding,' Barbara says. 'Want to hear it?'

Not really, just fuck off, he wants to snarl. But he says nothing and pushes himself tighter against the mirrored wall.

'Pease porridge hot, pease porridge cold, pease porridge in the pot, nine days old. Some like it hot, some like it cold, some like it in the pot, nine days old.'

'Could you hit the emergency button or something?' Paul says, impatiently.

'Which one's that?'

'I dunno, I can't see.'

'Neither can I.'

'Well feel for it, you're next to the panel.'

One by one, Paul watches as the rest of the buttons on the panel light up red – '2', '3', '4', '5', '6', '7' and '8'. Then '9' lights up green.

'Can't you find the emergency button?' he asks, his heart quickening even more. 'There's got to be one.'

'Sorry, there isn't. You're gonna have to go all the way to the top with me.' Barbara's voice is laced with something like malice, but not quite as bold. Whatever it is, he feels threatened.

'I need to get out. Now.'

'Sorry, that's not gonna happen. One day for each floor, that's how long it's gonna take. You're gonna spend nine days in this little pot with me, darl. Can't rush these things.'

'What are you talking about?'

'Nine days in the pot, weren't you listening?' Barbara chuckles. 'Some like it hot, some like it cold.'

'Are you still banging on about pease pudding?' The cloying stink of it rakes at the back of Paul's nose and he's much too aware of Barbara's hulking presence. The blackness all around him begins to beat red, as if it's organic. He's too hot. Undoes his top button. Doesn't like this blindness.

'See that ninth little circle?' Barbara says.

The '9' button is the odd one out, still glowing green.

Paul snorts more forced laughter. It sounds entirely too nervous. 'The ninth circle of Hell, you mean?'

'Ah, not just a funny guy, but startlingly bright too.' Barbara cackles. 'It'll take nine days to reach the ninth circle, and in that time, you'll have eaten all these sandwiches.'

'I guarantee you I won't.' Paul shakes his head, even though she can't see.

Can't she?

'Oh, but you will. I insist.'

'Not a chance I'm eating even one of your sandwiches, love.'

'Wanna bet?' Paul feels the pressure of the trolley digging into his thighs, so much so it hurts. 'You'll have fattened up nicely by the time we get to the ninth circle.'

Paul reaches down to shove the trolley away, feels stir crazy in this hellish confinement, but unexpected hot, meaty breath coats his face with a nearness that makes him flinch. He presses himself as much as he can against the back wall.

'When you're fat enough, I'm gonna slather you in pease pudding and gobble you up,' Barbara croons. A scaly, forklike tongue swipes across his cheek. 'You most certainly aren't getting out of here alive, darl.'

R. H. DIXON

Shoelace

Cheryl's heart pounds, an uncomfortable thrum, as she looks at herself in the mirror that's mounted on the wall next to the front door.

You look dreadful.

Nice try, but you can't sabotage my plan. Not this time.

She takes a deep breath. She's not checking her appearance. Doesn't particularly care if her hair is tidy or scarf is straight. She's simply addressing herself, checking the resolve in her eyes.

And it's there. She sees it. It's definitely there.

Good.

Very good.

Despite this edgy determination, the toast she'd eaten a short while ago churns in her stomach and her palms are sweaty. She wipes her hands down her jeans, then bends to adjust her left shoe. It's pinching at the sides and doesn't feel quite right.

Maybe it's just an excuse. You're stalling because you don't really want to go.

'I'm not stalling,' Cheryl says. 'If I don't adjust it, it'll cause blisters.'

Yeah, sure. Course it will.

She undoes the lace, tugs on the tongue so it sits more comfortably on the bridge of her foot, then pulls both ends of the lace to tighten. As she does, one end snaps off in her hand. She stares at the ragged edge of black cotton, feeling more upset than, perhaps, she should. She's been psyching herself up all week for this outing.

Has been cooped up too long and needs some fresh air, some outside stimulus. She was all ready to go.

But now this.

It's okay, the house says. *Stay with me. You don't need shoes here.*

'I need to go out.' Determined, Cheryl kicks off both shoes and stomps to the cupboard to get a different pair.

But why?

The house is her cosy, safe space, there's no doubt about that. It sings to her and, in response, she slow dances to its rhythm. She knows all its lines and edges and nuances of light and shade as the sun arcs from east to west. She knows its quiet spots and warm spots, and how each room feels depending on its moods.

Moods? Ha! See what you do to me?

'I need to get out of here,' she insists.

But why? I have ten rooms. There's so much you can do within them.

'They're not enough. I need more…'

Don't say that.

'But it's true. There's a whole world out there.'

How can you be so cruel? I thought I was your world?

'You are. I mean, you were. But lately I feel like a prisoner.'

The house gasps. *Is that how you truly feel?*

'Yes, so I really must go.' Cheryl's standing at the front door again with a pair of slip-on shoes grasped in her hands. She drops them to the floor and stuffs her feet inside.

But what if I show you the eleventh room? the house blurts when Cheryl grips the door handle, ready to leave.

'The eleventh room? What eleventh room?'

Oops.

'There can't be any other spaces that I don't already know about. There just can't be. It's not possible.'

The eleventh room is a secret and no one else can

know about it. If you promise you won't leave and not to tell anyone else, I'll show it to you. Only you.

Cheryl falters and sighs. She turns and looks into the mirror and sees her frightened reflection staring back.

Please, let's not do this. Just go.

But there's no hint of resolve left in her eyes.

Are you ready to see it?

'Okay, I'll stay.'

Good girl, the house says. *Now go and put those shoes in the bin. You won't need them again.*

Buttercup

Andrea clutches her bag in her lap as the Number 22 bounces over a speed bump. All about her, seats and railings rattle in their metal fixtures. There are twelve other people on the bus, including the driver. All passengers are seated, except a bare-legged girl who's standing in the aisle, twirling a buttercup between her fingers. The girl looks about eight, has straw-coloured hair and is wearing a pale yellow jacket over a pale pink dress. The outfit reminds Andrea of Battenburg cake; a childhood favourite of hers, which she's not had in such a long time.

Could easily pick some up next time I'm at the supermarket, Andrea thinks.

And maybe she will.

But maybe she won't.

Dark smudges beneath the girl's eyes accentuate a too-pale complexion. Andrea wonders if she's unwell. None of the other passengers seem in any way interested in or connected with the girl, so Andrea decides she'll keep an eye on her. It's an instinctive reaction. Andrea can't imagine her own daughter having travelled alone on public transport at such an age. There are too many weirdos about.

'Excuse me, would you like to know when you'll die?' the girl says to a nearby young couple, showing them her buttercup.

Andrea is taken aback. Isn't certain she heard correctly.

But maybe she did, because an old lady behind the

young couple shuffles forward in her seat and says, 'Buttercups are supposed to show if a person likes butter or not, dear.'

The girl's brow creases. 'What would be the point of that? You could just as easily ask if they do and save yourself the bother.' She shrugs. 'And unless I'm about to make sandwiches, which I'm not, why would I care?'

'It's just supposed to be a bit of fun.'

'Doesn't sound like any kind of fun to me.' The girl kneels on the seat in front of the young couple and, without being invited to, holds the buttercup beneath the young woman's chin. Her skin glows yellow. The girl smiles, evidently happy with this, and says, 'You'll die in your sleep when you're ninety-four.' She then moves her arm and holds the buttercup beneath the young man's chin. His skin glows yellow, too. 'And you'll live till you're eighty-eight. It won't be an easy death, but you'll be surrounded by family who love you.'

The young couple look at each other, eyebrows raised.

'Erm, okay,' says the young man. 'Thanks for that. I think.'

The girl nods. 'You're very welcome.' She stands again and moves to the old lady behind the young couple and holds the buttercup beneath her chin.

Andrea continues watching with mild interest and can see this time it casts a shadow. The girl must be doing something with her hand to create the effect, she thinks.

'You'll die a horrible death,' the girl says to the old lady. 'There'll be lots of icy, black water and you'll be trapped in a metal cage and your lungs will fill up till you can't breathe no more. It'll happen very soon.'

'Well,' the old lady admonishes, her mouth tightening in vexation. 'How impudent.'

'Yes, totally uncalled for,' says a middle-aged man across the way. 'That wasn't a very nice thing to say, young lady. You should apologise, you know.'

The girl shrugs. 'But it's true. Why should I be sorry?' She holds the buttercup beneath the middle-aged man's chin.

Still watching, and slightly dumbfounded, Andrea sees how the flower casts a shadow, too deep and dark, on the middle-aged man's chin.

'You'll die soon too,' the girl tells him. 'You'll be bashed about like a doll and there'll be lots of blood and broken bones and smashed glass and screaming. It'll be truly awful. Worse than anything that's ever happened to you before.'

'I suppose you think you're funny?' the middle-aged man says, squaring his shoulders, clearly ruffled. He looks about and asks, 'Is anyone with this young girl?'

No one speaks up.

The girl simply regards him, her expression vacant.

The young couple stands, and the young woman presses the button to sound the bell to let the bus driver know they'd like to get off at the next stop. As they move towards the door, the girl walks further up the aisle, bringing her ill-omened buttercup and grisly imagination closer to Andrea.

Andrea's heart begins to pound.

She chastises herself for being ridiculous.

It's just a kid, for crying out loud. A bored kid, at that.

And yet she considers jumping up and getting off the bus with the young couple because she doesn't want to hear how she might die, nor how soon. Something about this kid, this bus ride...

But the idea is founded on nothing but silliness and she's nowhere near home, so Andrea stays seated. Mustn't get worked up.

The bus stops with a shuddering sigh and the young couple disembark. Andrea watches out the window as they take each other's hand and stroll away.

Lucky them.

She thinks of her husband, Mark, and wishes he was with her now. He'd nudge her arm and grin and say, Who's this creepy kid, eh? And she'd laugh and tell him to shush and wouldn't feel at all nervous. Because when they're together, nothing else matters. But right now, he's miles away at work, and she's on this bus.

'Excuse me, would you like to know when you'll die?' the girl asks.

Andrea realises with dread that the question is being aimed at her. She turns her head and finds the girl's light green, almost yellow, eyes are fixed on her. They're a sickly colour, and Andrea shrinks away from them as much as the question itself, edging closer to the window and shaking her head. 'That's very kind, but I'd rather not know. Thanks.'

The girl simply smiles and nods, then moves away.

Andrea's chest heaves with relief. She hadn't expected to get off so easily. Kids are persistent, after all.

Hey ma, watch me do this thing I'm about to do.

You're not watching.

Ma, watch me.

Watch!

The doors hiss closed, and the bus judders on its way again, passing the young couple and leaving them behind to a lifetime together – or not. It's late afternoon and the low winter sun catches the surface of the approaching river. The glare dazzles Andrea, causing a fiery white orb to spoil her field of vision.

She closes her eyes and thinks of a happy memory; she's with Mark and the kids and the dogs and they're all at the beach together, the dogs running, all of them being noisy and...

'Excuse me, would you like to know when you'll die?' the girl asks a man two seats behind Andrea.

The man sighs, acting put out, but says, 'Go on then, if you must.'

In her peripheral vision, the bit not blinded by the sun's glare on black water, Andrea sees the girl hold the buttercup to the man's chin. She doesn't know if it glows yellow or if the flower casts a shadow.

'You'll die soon,' the girl says.

Andrea imagines the man's chin is black.

'Well, aren't you a little ray of sunshine?' the man says.

There's no hint of mischief in the girl's tone when she tells him, 'You'll be crushed to death.'

The man snorts. 'Oh yeah? By what?'

'See that lorry?' The girl points to the windscreen.

Beyond the fading orb that continues to haunt both of her retinas, Andrea sees a lorry approaching in the distance up ahead.

'What about it?' the man asks.

'Keep watching, you'll see.'

The lorry swerves, then rights itself.

Andrea grips the seat in front, her heart beating faster.

'The lorry driver's been on the road for hours and hours without taking a break,' the girl says. 'He's about to fall asleep and lose control of the lorry and the bus driver won't see till it's too late because the sun's in his eyes and he's distracted. The lorry will smash into the bus, and we'll spin round and fly right off the side of the bridge and into the river.'

'If that's true, then why don't you do something to stop it from happening?' the man says. He's acting blasé-bold, cocky even, yet there's an edge to his voice that betrays his mild unease. Because who is this kid with her macabre predictions and why is no one with her and why does what she say seem so unnervingly real, like all of it might happen?

'Them's not the rules,' the girl says. 'It has to be this way.'

'Hey, bus driver!' the man shouts. 'Watch out for that

lorry up ahead, yeah?'

The bus driver turns his head. 'What's that you say?'

The girl laughs.

'Stop distracting him,' Andrea says, panic welling up inside of her. She watches as the lorry swerves again, crossing onto their side of the road.

'Everything alright back there?' the bus driver calls, his head still turned.

The girl smiles. 'You'll all die together. Isn't that nice?'

'No,' Andrea says. 'Because it's not my time.'

'I'm afraid if fate says it's time, it's time,' the girl answers, twirling the buttercup in her fingers.

'But you didn't check if it's my time. So, you can't possibly know when I'm supposed to die.'

The girl looks troubled by this challenge. She moves towards Andrea, her arm outstretched, ready with the buttercup. But Andrea snatches the flower from the girl's fingers and puts it in her mouth.

The girl's expression morphs into one of horror. 'What are you doing?'

Andrea chews, then swallows.

The girl and the bus and all its passengers dissolve, and Andrea finds she's standing on a beach. The sand, pale grains like smashed glass ground to powder, stretches on for miles and miles in all directions, and she can't see the sea. It's a crude black line in her head, lurking beyond the horizon like a monster hiding. She thinks if she could see it, it would scream loudly. The sun is a burnt white orb in an anaemic sky. She can hear voices and dogs barking.

Andrea turns and sees two dogs – her dogs – racing towards her. Behind them are two figures, waving. Could be her son and daughter. Only they seem too small, like they're younger than they should be. But they're way off in the distance, so it's probably an illusion.

'Hi there,' she calls to them, waving. 'Hurry.'

'Hey, love.' Mark's standing right next to her. He's grinning, and his eyes reflect the burnt orb of the sun too much, making him look somehow different. She's pleased to see him, even though she isn't sure how he approached without her noticing.

'Thought we might have a picnic,' he says, taking a backpack from his shoulder.

Andrea smiles. She has a funny taste in her mouth and feels strange. She can't remember getting here or what she was doing beforehand. 'Why aren't you at work?'

Mark frowns. 'Don't you want us to have a picnic?'

'Of course, but…'

'Right then.' Mark unzips the backpack and shows its contents to her.

Inside, in individual cellophane wrappers, are thick wedges of Battenburg cake.

Pink and yellow.

Nothing else.

'No sandwiches?' Andrea asks.

'Wasn't sure if you like butter or not,' Mark says, shrugging. 'Couldn't remember.'

And she finds it strange that he doesn't remember.

But there's something she can't quite remember as well.

So his not remembering if she likes butter doesn't seem so bad.

It really doesn't matter.

The dogs arrive, scurrying around her legs, kicking up sand. Andrea bends to fuss them, happy they're here even though there's something different about them, but not. They're the wrong shade, perhaps. Different shape?

Hey, ma! The kids shout. Watch us do this thing we're about to do.

Mark hands Andrea a slice of cake.

'We'll all eat together,' he says. 'Isn't this nice?'
And she thinks it is.
Except the taste in her mouth.
And there's something else…
But she can't think straight.
Ma, you're not watching!

Frog

Kath's still in her pyjamas, playing a word game on her smartphone and eating cereal at the breakfast bar, when a call comes through from her boss. She stares at the screen for a couple of seconds, then sighs. Accepting the call, she presses the device to her ear and says, 'John?'

'Any chance you can get to work?'

Kath looks at the wall clock above the fridge. 'My shift starts in less than an hour, I'll be there soon enough.'

'But I need you here five minutes ago.'

Kath rolls her eyes. John's prone to being dramatic. 'Why? What's up?'

'Something has happened, I can't explain. It's weird. I need you to take a look. Can you please just get here pronto?'

Kath feels it's not so much of a question than a command. Either way, her interest is piqued, so she leaves the remainder of her cornflakes on the counter, throws on some clothes and hurries to the office where she finds John waiting for her, pacing at the door.

'What's going on?' Kath drops her bag onto her desk, thinking: It'd better be good.

'Fire it up,' John says, pointing at Kath's desktop. 'And go to the company's homepage.'

They wait an excruciating five minutes for Kath's ancient machine to boot up, John still refusing to tell her what the problem is because she must see it for herself, apparently. He further adds to the air of suspense he's created with copious amounts of impatient finger tapping and sighing.

As it is, turns out the company's website has been hacked. John hangs over Kath's shoulder, breathing coffee-breath onto her neck, as they watch small, pixelated frogs fall from the top of the screen in a constant stream, making the company homepage's content impossible to read.

'See,' he says, touching the screen with his finger as if to further validate the cartoon frogs. 'They're everywhere.'

'Well, first of all, let's not panic,' Kath says, irked by the blurry mark his finger has left on her screen. 'There's no sensitive information linked to the website, so there's nothing that could have been stolen and used. At worst, it'll be a time-consuming nuisance to fix.' Certainly not worth having dragged me away from my cornflakes for, she thinks. You owe me a pint, matey.

'But why frogs?'

'Why not?'

'But why?'

'I don't know, John. I really don't know.' Kath opens Google Chrome and is about to search for any information on animated frog graphics that relate to hackers, when Annette, John's secretary, pops her head into the office and says, 'Kath, you know how you showed me how to upload pictures onto our Facebook thingy?'

'Facebook page?'

'Yeah, that. Well, when you get a minute, can you come and have a look at what I've done?'

'I'm kind of busy at the moment, Annette. What have you done?'

'I dunno. I think I might have broken something.'

'Broken what?'

'Everything.'

'You think you've broken Facebook?'

'Yeah.'

'I can assure you, you haven't broken Facebook.'

Annette winces. 'But I tried to upload a new picture and suddenly there were all these frogs on the screen and...'

'Frogs?' Kath and John say at the same time.

'Yeah. Little green frogs tumbling from the top of the screen.'

'On Facebook, you say?' John asks.

'Yeah.'

Kath's mobile jingles with a breaking news alert. She retrieves it from her bag and activates the screen. A red banner with white text says: GLOBAL ATTACK: SOCIAL MEDIA HACKED BY FROGS

'Wow,' she says. 'This is bigger than I thought.'

'Was it something I pressed?' Annette asks.

Kath sighs, resisting an eye roll. 'I know you have your moments, like the time you wiped out the entire shared drive. But no, Annette, you didn't break Facebook, this issue is worldwide. No offence, but you're not nearly savvy enough to be able do that.'

Annette exhales in a show of relief. 'As long as you're sure.'

'I'm sure.'

'Right then, anyone for a cuppa?'

Kath and John both answer affirmatively.

'At least it's not just us,' John says, walking to the window, his shoulders less tense already.

'I think it'd be preferable if it was just us,' Kath says. 'We're small fries on the face of it. It would have been fixable. As it is, this is potentially massive. Who knows what it could mean for everyone.'

'But it's someone else's problem to fix now, isn't it?' John says, with a wink, as if he's two steps ahead of her.

It's not like it would have been you doing the fixing anyway, Kath wants to point out, but doesn't. Instead, she says, 'I suppose. But if all our personal information in the digital ether has been jeopardised, I'd say this is most people's problem to worry about. Everyone and their granny is on social media just about. And who's to say this amphibious virus will stop at social media?'

'Aren't frogs reptilian?'

'Are you being serious?'

John shrugs. 'Like I said, it's someone else's problem.' He switches on the retro-looking radio that sits on the sill just in time for a local radio presenter to announce: 'News just in. Following worldwide cybersecurity attacks in what's being dubbed Frog-gate, which comes just one day after the AI summit where some of the world's top technological geniuses met to discuss the advances and implications of artificial intelligence, worrying reports are coming in about major disruptions on the A1 between Newcastle and Chester-le-Street. It appears there's been a sudden down-pouring of frogs. Yes, that's right, just as our social media screens are pouring with frogs, it's raining actual frogs outside, folks. They're filling the motorway and…'

The radio crackles and the station is lost.

'Frigging hell, is this a late April Fools' or something?' John fiddles with the radio's knob, tuning into a different station where a broadcaster is saying, 'Reports are coming in thick and fast from around the world that frogs are literally falling from the sky…'

The radio goes dead again.

Kath notices the room has become gloomy; a grainy darkness that's too much like dusk. She joins John by the window and looks up. The sky is a shifting mass, angry and bruised looking.

'Reckon we'll get a downpouring of frogs here?' John says, still fiddling with the radio's knob.

'It certainly looks that way.'

The first frog hits the pavement outside of their office

at 9:22. Kath and John stay by the window and watch as thousands more follow. The frogs are unusually large, and don't splatter when they hit the ground. They keep coming. More and more of them.

The radio hisses loudly, then sizzles to silence. Neither Kath nor John tries to retune it.

'Crikey, look at it out there,' John says, his breath fogging the window. 'What are we supposed to do?'

Kath shrugs. What is there to do? 'Stay inside.'

'But what about when we need to go home?'

'Let's cross that bridge when we come to it. It's certainly not an option now, is it?'

'Let's hope the council has it all cleared by five, eh?'

'Cleared?' Kath raises an eyebrow. 'Using what?'

'I dunno.' John shakes his head. 'Snow ploughs? Tractors? Anything that could scoop the frogs up in large batches to be dumped.'

'Dumped where?'

'The countryside? The sea? I don't really care, it's not my problem.'

'I think you'll find it is. Besides, there's an awful lot of frogs out there, John. Who exactly in the council is going to undertake this task you've assigned?'

'Refuse collectors? I've no idea, but they'll have to do something about it. That's why I pay my council tax.'

'I'm pretty sure council tax doesn't cover biblical downpourings of frogs. Hell, we pay extra to have our garden waste collected. We're in unchartered territory, here.'

'The army then, that's who'll sort it. They'll be drafted in, just you watch.'

'Sounds like it's a global problem, so the whole of our tiny country is probably covered with frogs by now. Where would the army even start? I guess we'll just have to see how things pan out.' To make light of the situation, which Kath, for the record, doesn't find remotely funny, she adds, 'Suppose it could have rained much worse things though, eh?'

The door to the office opens and Annette appears, carrying a tray of tea and biscuits. She sets it down on Kath's desk and says, 'Are frogs supposed to have teeth?'

Kath's brow furrows. Immediately, she doesn't like where this might lead. Something about Annette's expression unsettles her. 'Er, yes, I believe so. How come?'

'Big ones?'

'No, a row of tiny ones on their upper jaw, I think.'

'Well, there's one of those big frogs from outside in the kitchen, near the sink. When I went to fill the kettle, it hissed and bared its teeth at me, and its teeth most definitely weren't tiny.'

Kath scrunches her eyes and groans. 'Is it just the one frog in there?'

'I'm not sure. I think so?'

'How on earth did it get there?' John asks.

'The window's open.'

'And who left the bloody window open?' John throws his arms in the air and marches from the room. 'For chrissakes, Annette, we don't want the place to be overrun with frogs. You need to start using your loaf, woman.'

'But I didn't open it,' Annette says to Kath, as they listen to their boss's footsteps echo down the corridor. 'John opens it every morning as soon as he gets in, even when it's colder than a witch's tit outside. Honestly, you'd think he's menopausal.'

The radio bursts to life with another deafening hiss.

'Bloomin' heck, that's loud,' Annette says, startled.

Kath turns the radio's knob till the hissing stops. 'It's been acting up all morning. Maybe it's the frogs interfering with the signal.'

'Creepy,' Annette says. 'It was almost as though there were voices in amongst all that hissing.'

'Voices?'

As if on cue, a new voice comes through with crystal clear clarity: 'Attention all, this is a nationwide safety alert. With immediate effect, you are advised to stay indoors and keep your doors and windows closed. The frogs are reported to be highly dangerous and will attack and bite when in proximity. We have reason to believe they carry a deadly virus, one that can be passed from person to person once a person becomes infected. So, I repeat, keep your windows and doors closed and do not go outside.'

Kath and Annette stare at each other in disbelief.

'Shit, it sounds like Covid all over again, only worse,' Kath says.

'Hmmm, he didn't sound quite right.' Annette says, taking a seat. 'Don't you think?'

'In what way?' Kath notices the green frogs on her computer screen have now changed. They're black with toxic skull symbols on their chests.

'He sounded a bit too, I dunno, robotic? Like the gadgety thingummy Bob's got set up at home. The virtual assistant. You know, ask it a question and it knows the answer.' Annette's eyes narrow. 'Only, that voice on the radio sounded... smug?'

And now she thinks about it, Kath thinks Annette is right and her thoughts start to spiral. 'Do you think all of this somehow follows on from the AI summit yesterday?'

'What's AI?'

'Artificial intelligence. Like the gadgety thingummy Bob has set up in your house, only it's often way, way cleverer than that.'

'So what are you suggesting?'

'Maybe AI has intercepted the radio waves to deliver

panic-inducing messages to the world. It could certainly be responsible for the cyberattack.'

'What about the frogs outside?'

'I dunno. Could AI have orchestrated a storm of mutant, deadly frogs to fall from the sky?'

'If it's so intelligent, as you say, then I don't see why not.'

'But why?'

Annette shakes her head. 'There's no good reason that I can think of.'

Kath's mouth is suddenly dry. 'Oh God. Biowarfare.'

From elsewhere in the building there comes a scream; a terrible wail that makes Kath and Annette flinch.

'Quick!' Annette jumps to her feet. 'We should barricade the door so John can't get back in.'

'But why?'

'Because he might have been bitten which means he'll have the deadly virus and I don't want to die.'

'But what if he hasn't been bitten?' Kath stares on, bewildered as Annette wedges a chair beneath the handle of the door. 'We don't even know if the radio broadcast was genuine, and if the frogs are indeed deadly.'

'I'm not willing to take that risk. I have grandkids.'

'I have kids.'

'So, think about them.'

There's a distant thump.

John falling to the floor?

Kath imagines him struggling beneath a horde of blood-thirsty frogs. 'Seriously, Annette, you can't just leave him out there.'

Annette folds her arms and narrows her eyes. 'Watch me.'

'John?' Kath shouts. 'Are you okay?'

He doesn't respond, but there's a new rhythmic sound in the corridor.

Wet hands slapping the floor as John drags his body

closer?

Wet hands?

Kath's thoughts turn red.

She takes a step towards the door, but Annette stands in the way and says, 'Don't come any closer, Kath. I'm warning you.'

'Calm down, eh?' Kath says, inching further forward.

'I like you, I really do.' Annette lifts the small fire extinguisher from its bracket on the wall. 'But I swear to God I'll smash your fucking brains out if you try to let him back in here.'

'Christ, Annette, let's not be dramatic.'

There's a tapping at the window. Two frogs on the window's outside ledge are banging their heads against the glass pane. The force is not enough to break the glass, Kath thinks, but there are thousands more frogs surrounding the building. How long before they infiltrate it.

'I can't stand this,' Annette says, her chest heaving as she starts to cry. 'This is crazy. Why is this happening?'

The radio erupts with cackling laughter that's completely digital and not at all human. Then Freddie Mercury's voice fills the room: I Want to Break Free.

Battle

Marian's standing with her face tilted to the sky. The night is still. Too still. It lends a staged quality to her surroundings as though she's on a film set. The moon hides behind a blanket of cloud, pitching this familiar yet unfamiliar field into obscurity. She's never been here before, except in the pages of history books.

What would it have been like on the eve before the battle? Deathly still, like it is now? No wind or rain to cause a nuisance and dampen the terror of around 7,000 men. Their death-marching thoughts amplified, hanging in the stagnant air.

A distant, soundless thunder reverberates through the ground. Marian feels it coursing through the soles of her shoes. Or does she merely imagine it?

She continues to stand still.

She's not here on a ghost-hunt, she wants to absorb the atmosphere of the place itself, feels a connection with it. Needs time to reflect on all the carnage that unfolded so she can explore the aftermath and how it feels now.

It's important that she knows.

Can peace and hope exist where such horror once reigned?

She must know.

The darkness is insidious, and a large, black shape rushes past to her right.

A man on a horse?

Marian twirls round, but there's no one there.

Shifting clouds causing shadows to stir?

Most likely.

But the thundering that travels through the earth is now audible, growing louder and louder, frightening in its enormity.

Hundreds of hooves crashing towards her, bringing forth a ghostly battalion?

Marian's heart beats faster.

The battlefield of Battle is starting to deliver. It's remembering the past.

But what comes after?

Marian scrunches her hands into fists.

She stands firm. Scared, but ready.

It's important that she knows.

Magic

The rain's coming down, relentless and heavy. Dean pulls over at the side of the road because the windscreen wipers can't keep up. The road ahead is nothing but an obscure blur of grey. Sat Nav stopped working a while ago. Dean has no idea where he is, apart from somewhere in Cumbria. He's supposed to meet Martyn Smith, an old school friend, and some friends of Martyn's he's not yet met, for a weekend of outdoor activities. Eleven was the agreed meeting time, in the car park of The Jolly Rambler. It's ten-thirty now. He's almost certainly going to be late. Can't even call Martyn to let him know he's lost, as his phone has no signal.

Dean sighs.

Bloody weather.

It's the Lake District, so he supposes rain like this must be typical, but there's something unsettling about this downpour's ferocity. The way it pounds the car makes it sound like it's being pelted with stones. He imagines the silver metalwork might well be pitted. Dean can't remember the last time he saw a house, or another car for that matter. He hasn't seen any road signs in a long while either. So, he waits in the car on a grassy verge, checking his phone every couple of minutes in case it picks up a signal.

It doesn't.

He waits some more.

It takes around an hour for the rain to ease. By now the windows are steamed. Dean turns the key in the ignition and cracks open the driver's side window, then watches as the fog on the glass slowly clears.

The road ahead doesn't look at all what he'd expected. It's a long, straight stretch that goes as far into the distance as he can see; nondescript flat, green land to either side and an unknown grey mountain range its promised destination. Until now it's been all winding, narrow roads edged by trees and bushes and charming stone walls, so Dean worries he might not even be in Cumbria anymore.

He checks his phone again. Still no signal.

Best get going.

Dean drives off, resolving to stop at the next house, shop or petrol station to ask for directions. Only, he doesn't encounter any of those things. On and on he goes, increasing in speed till he's doing eighty. He feels reckless speeding on an unknown road, but also worried enough to not let up on the accelerator. The grey mountains in the distance don't seem to get any closer, and the road ahead is still just as long. Something at the side of the road ahead catches Dean's attention. Something white with a blotch of red on it.

A sheep?

Dean slows. If it's a sheep surely there must be a farm nearby. This thought inspires a smidgen of hope that the outdoorsy weekend painstakingly planned by Martyn might not be a write-off after all. Dean's flutter of hope is soon dashed, however, when he sees it's not a sheep, but a white rock with a red spray-painted greater-than symbol on it. Dean cruises past the white rock without stopping and realises the grey mountains, perhaps darker now, are still no closer. And there's a strong sense of foreboding that crawls over his skin with insect legs and fills all the empty spaces in the car. Dean's so tense, his neck hurts.

Something isn't right.

Around five minutes later, another white shape appears

in the distance; a white rock at the side of the road with a red greater-than symbol painted on its surface. Dean slows to a crawl, staring at it suspiciously because he thinks it looks very much like the white rock he'd passed before. Ahead, the grey mountains are still no closer.

Dean glances in the rear-view mirror. There are no mountains back there, just road and sky. He catches a glimpse of his own nervous eyes staring back and shivers. An overwhelming sense of being watched encourages him to put his foot down on the accelerator, and off he speeds again.

Another five minutes pass, then Dean sees another white shape in the distance. He grips the steering wheel, arms stiff. It's another white rock with the same red greater-than symbol sprayed on it.

I don't like this, he thinks. I don't like this at all.

He pulls over. Can't shake the feeling it's the exact same rock he's seen twice before. After some deliberation, Dean grabs his coffee flask from the centre console and gets out of the car. It's warmer outside than he'd imagined, humid even. His bare arms tingle with gooseflesh as though the air is thick with static. Probably thunder rolling in. The air smells of rain and something else he can't quite place. It's a cloying stink that's nauseating and sweet. Dean balances his empty flask on top of the white rock. There's no risk of it blowing over, he thinks, as it's eerily still out. No breeze at all.

No sound either.

Nothing.

'I don't like this,' Dean says aloud, before hurrying back to the car. He drives off, intermittently checking his flask in the rear-view mirror till he can no longer see it.

After around five minutes, just as he expects, another white shape appears up ahead. Dean's heart speeds up. He's almost too afraid to get any closer to the white rock, because what if...

Yep. There's his flask sitting on top, right where he'd left it.

Dean pulls over, his hands now shaking.

He's been driving in a straight loop. How is that possible?

He considers the greater-than symbol on the rock.

Is it, perhaps, directing him to travel the other way?

It's pointing in the direction from which he's come, after all.

'Alright then, let's go back.' Dean grips the steering wheel, ready to turn the car round, because he can't continue down this road. It's insane.

As he does, however, a small figure steps from behind the white rock.

'Wanna see some magic, mister?' It's a boy of around eight in blue jeans and a white t-shirt. His face is puckered and waxy where his eyes should be but aren't. A fleshy mountain range that looks like old wounds. Old and violent.

Dean rolls down his window but doesn't reply. He simply stares.

The boy moves closer. 'Well, do you?'

'No, I don't. I just want to get out of here.'

The boy shrugs. 'Do you want your flask back?'

Dean shakes his head. Then remembers the kid is blind, so tells him, 'No.'

The boy points to the grey mountains in the distance, the mountains which are no closer than they were fifteen minutes ago, and says, 'When it comes, if it sees you first, you're dead meat.'

'When what comes?'

'You'll have to see it to know. But you'll know when you see it.'

'Huh?'

'Even if you see it first though, mister, that's not the end of it. If you see it five times or more, you're even worse than dead meat. So don't say you've not been warned.'

'What does that mean? Is it a riddle?'

'Maybe.' The boy smiles revealing teeth that are too small. Ground down, perhaps. Something about him is utterly terrifying. 'Are you sure you don't wanna see some magic?'

'What kind of magic?'

The boy clicks his fingers and vanishes.

Dean stares at the space where the boy was but now isn't.

The weird smell from outside has infiltrated the car with a chemical stink that's dizzying.

Dean's sweating but can't stop shivering. He rolls the window up, spins the car round so he's facing the way he'd come, slams his foot down on the accelerator and speeds off. Jittery, he keeps checking the rear-view mirror expecting the boy to reappear.

He doesn't. For which Dean is pleased.

Not my problem, he tells himself.

Isn't it? His conscience niggles.

No, I've got places to be. Things to do. I don't have time for this craziness.

He keeps driving. Feels a little unhinged. Guilty for fleeing, but also not. It's not long till he sees a familiar white shape up ahead. The sight of it makes him issue a strangled shriek from the back of his throat because something's so terribly wrong about it, it defies logic, and he can't possibly begin to understand. The white rock is on the wrong side of the road.

The wrong side!

Before he'd turned the car, the repetition of the white rock was to Dean's right. Now, by rights, it should be to his left. But it's not.

It's not.

How can this be?

And, perhaps, to contradict this impossibility, thus making things weirder than they already are, Dean realises the painted red sign on the white rock is now a lesser-than symbol.

nononononononononononononononono

Dean slaps his face. His palm smarts against his cheek, causing a sharp sting that would wake him if he was stuck in an awful dream.

But he's not dreaming.

This is real.

He's driving and he speeds past the white rock without stopping, pretending he hasn't seen it.

What else can he do?

Tap-tap-tap.

A muffled sound emanates from somewhere within the car.

Tap-tap-tap.

Sounds like it's coming from the boot. Dean ignores it. Tells himself something must have shaken loose from his overnight bag and is rattling about back there. It's the easiest, safest reasoning.

Does he believe it?

Tap-tap-tap. Tap-tap-tap.

No.

'Shut up,' he says, imagining the creepy boy with no eyes has materialised in the boot, intent on tormenting him. 'I'm not listening, so bugger off.'

Tap-tap-tap. Tap-tap-tap. Tap-tap-tap. Tap-tap-tap. Tap-tap-tap. Tap-tap-tap.

'Shut. Up!'

Tap-tap-tap. Tap-tap-tap. Tap-tap-tap. Tap-tap-tap.

If he doesn't check inside the boot, Dean thinks his sanity will untether itself from whatever holds it in place. So he brakes hard, doesn't even bother to pull over onto the grass verge, because what's the point? No one else is using this awful stretch of road.

Everything looks normal and as it should in the boot. His overnight bag is zipped and secure. Nothing has broken free to roll about. Dean scratches his head. He thinks he sees the canvas fabric of the overnight bag shift ever so slightly, as though something inside it moved. He unzips the bag and roots about, shifting his clothes and toiletries aside, unsure what he expects to find. The bag's certainly not big enough for the boy with no eyes to fit inside. As it is, he finds nothing untoward.

Perhaps the knocking had come from beneath the car. A mechanical fault?

Great, just what I need.

He closes the boot, then gets back into the car to continue his journey.

And it's not long till he sees another (the) white rock up ahead. He doesn't know if he's relieved or not to see that the boy with no eyes is sitting on top of it. The boy's head is turned, cocked, tracking the sound of the oncoming car.

Not my responsibility, Dean thinks. Not my problem.

He drives past without stopping. When he flashes a glance at the rear-view mirror, he sees the boy raise the flask in the air as though making a toast.

'It's coming,' the boy shouts. 'Make sure you see it first!'

'What's coming?' Dean is sweating profusely and, 'Jesus Christ,' it's only now he realises the grey mountains are all wrong. They're in front of him.

How can this be?

He checks the rear-view mirror and sees only road and sky behind, no mountains.

This isn't right. None of it's right.

He turns the car again, but as soon as he does the grey mountains are ahead and, reflected in the rear-view mirror, there's nothing but road and sky.

'Fuck!' Tears of frustration prick Dean's eyes. He

stops the car and gets out. 'What am I supposed to do?' he shouts up at the sky.

The grey mountains are even darker now, smudged charcoal peaks, and there's a menace emanating from them that's almost palpable.

'What am I supposed to do?'

A tapping sound comes from the rear end of the car. The same infuriating noise as before. Storming to the boot, Dean flings it open. His overnight bag moves. Surely no trick of his imagination. This time when he unzips it, a white rabbit jumps out. Dean flinches, as though the rabbit is dangerous. And maybe it is. Cringing, he grabs hold of it by the scruff of the neck, its fur silky-soft, and puts it on the road. Doesn't want it in his car.

Immediately, the rabbit hops about. Uninterested in Dean, it noses the ground.

Dean gets back into the car and turns it again. The grey mountains are still ahead and there's nothing behind. He issues a small cry. He's not even sure which way he was heading in the first place.

Does it even matter?

He resolves to drive nonstop till he arrives somewhere else that's not here. Jamming his foot on the accelerator, it's not long till he surpasses eighty. The landscape to either side is a complete blur.

Ninety.

The grey mountains ahead are still no closer.

One hundred.

'Come on, come on!'

One hundred and ten.

Dean laughs manically.

One hundred and twenty.

The car feels strained, but he won't let up. Must keep going.

Faster and faster.

Up ahead the white rock approaches.
The boy with no eyes is sitting on it.
Must keep going.
Faster and faster.
Up ahead the white rock approaches.
His flask is balanced on top.
Must keep going.
Faster and faster.
Up ahead the white rock approaches.
The white rabbit from his overnight bag is poised upright on it, front paws held aloft as it sniffs the air.
Must keep going.
Faster and faster.
Up ahead the white rock approaches.
The boy with no eyes is standing on it, on his head is a headband with white fluffy rabbit's ears.
Must keep going.
Faster and faster.
Up ahead the white rock approaches.
There's nothing on it.
Must keep going.
Faster and faster.
Up ahead the white rock approaches.
There's a small, bloodied white pelt draped on it.
Must keep going.
Faster and faster.
Up ahead the white rock approaches.
There's nothing on it. But the white rabbit is in the middle of the road and if it doesn't move, he's going to hit it.
Dean blasts his horn.
It doesn't move.
It doesn't move.
It doesn't move.
It doesn't move.
Dean swerves. Loses control of the car. It veers

violently and hits the white rock and the airbag is deployed and there's an awful, deafening metallic clang that might have dulled the sound of his nose rupturing. His skull splitting. His neck bones smashing. He closes his eyes. Glass sprays everywhere as the car's windows shatter upon impact. The noise of the crash stays lodged in Dean's head for minutes afterwards, his ears ring with the violence of it all. When the car doesn't explode in a ball of fire, he groans and fiddles with the seatbelt clasp, surprised he can move. It clicks free. Not caring about glass particles, he crawls through the wrecked window to his side, slithering down onto the grass verge. He feels adrenalized, but unharmed. There's no pain. Not yet.

The white rabbit watches from its place on the road.

The car's bonnet looks like an accordion.

The white rock sits unmoved.

The grey mountains in the distance are no closer.

There's a knife on top of the white rock, Dean sees. He staggers to his feet and picks it up. It's a stainless steel kitchen knife, its handle foreign and cold in his hand. But he feels better for having it. He starts walking away from the car, away from the mountains. His breathing is ragged, but his body isn't broken. He walks for fifteen minutes straight, refusing to look back. He feels hopeful when he realises he should have reached the white rock by now but hasn't. Risking a look back, he expects to see the grey mountains further away. But they're not. He hasn't moved at all. His smashed car, the white rock and the white rabbit are still right behind him as though he's been walking on a treadmill this whole time.

And what's that?

Dean can see something in the distance, pouring from the grey mountains. Something dark and awful and…

Oh.

God.

Oh…

You'll have to see it to know, the boy had said. But you'll know when you see it.

And somehow Dean knows.

When it comes, if it sees you first, you're dead meat.

'Well, I saw you first, you bastard,' Dean whimpers, as if this declaration will make it so. Really, he has no idea. He doesn't even know what the swirling, black mass is or if it has eyes.

If you see it five times or more, you're even worse than dead meat.

Dean turns and hangs his head and starts to jog, so he can't see the thing behind. Yet he has a strong urge to take another look because…

Because…

Because it's there and he needs to be certain that what he saw he really saw as he's not seen anything like it before and he can't say for sure it can logically exist and…

He turns his head and sees it again.

Oh God.

That's twice. You've seen it twice now.

Dean starts jogging, but he can't tell if he's moving or not and he doesn't know if the thing is following him.

'This isn't fair!'

He turns his head and sees it's even closer and blacker and more awful and filled with teeth and...

That's three times.

Dean's hyperventilating now. He stops running, can't decide what to do. A great shadow befalls the land all around him and there's a drop in temperature.

He looks up and sees the black mass above him.

That's four times.

And what if I blink?

Will that make it five?

Oh God.

It's stretching downwards, its yawning mouth ready to

swallow him.

And if it does?

Dean takes the knife and stabs at his eyes.

'Ha, I can't see you anymore,' he screams. 'I win. I win!' He lies on the ground and tries to flatten himself to the road. He waits for the terrible maw to crunch his body between its teeth.

Nothing happens.

He feels raindrops on his face.

Silky-soft fur against his hand that's still clutching the knife.

Solace in his sticky blindness.

'You're part of my magic show now, mister,' the boy with no eyes says from somewhere that's dark. Then he laughs.

Acknowledgements

Special thanks to Marian Bainbridge, Paul Gutridge, Andrea Illingworth, Mark Illingworth, Heather Kelly, Kirsty Lenaghan, Cheryl Middlemass, Kath Roebuck, Dean Setters and Dave Smith for sharing my enthusiasm and making this project fun. I hope you'll enjoy reading the tweaked stories within these pages. Each of you is now a character within a published story. Pretty cool, huh?

For the sake of copyright and not wanting to get into any kind of trouble for publishing other people's words, I've left the first lines of all the radio songs that were linked to each story out of the collection. You'll just have to trust me when I say it was an eclectic mix.

The second batch of radio-prompt stories, Uppercut & Other Stories, will follow on from this collection and complete the project. I'm hugely grateful for all those who took part and feature in the second volume and will thank you all individually within its depraved pages. You know who you are!

About The Author

R. H. Dixon is a horror enthusiast who, when not escaping into the fantastical realms of fiction, lives in the northeast of England with her husband and their whippet, Delilah.

Visit her website for horror features, short stories, promotions and news of her upcoming books: **www.rhdixon.com**

Printed in Great Britain
by Amazon